MONROE TALES

IT'S NOT GOODBYE, IT'S SEE YOU LATER

MONROE TALES

IT'S NOT GOODBYE, IT'S SEE YOU LATER

WRITTEN BY
SCHUYLER CROY

ILLUSTRATED BY GAY EZZI

Indigo River Publishing
3 West Garden Street Ste. 352 M
Pensacola, FL 32502
www.indigoriverpublishing.com

Ordering Information:
Quantity sales: Special discounts are available on quantity purchases by corporations, associations, and others. For details, contact the publisher at the address above.

Orders by U.S. trade bookstores and wholesalers: Please contact the publisher at the address above.

Printed in the United States of America
Illustrator: Gay Ezzi
Book Design: mycustombookcover.com
Editor: Justyn Newman

Library of Congress Control Number: 2018938886

ISBN: 978-1-948080-21-7

First Edition

With Indigo River Publishing, you can always expect great books, strong voices, and meaningful messages. Most importantly, you'll always find ... words worth reading.

THANK YOU TO THOSE WHO HAVE SERVED AND
ARE CURRENTLY SERVING.

A SPECIAL THANKS TO RWC FOR INSPIRING ME.

IT'S NOT GOODBYE, IT'S SEE YOU LATER.

THAT IS WHAT I KEEP BEING TOLD.

GOODBYE MEANS FOREVER BUT YOU ARE
NOT GOING TO BE GONE THAT LONG.

SOME DAYS WILL BE HARD AND DRAG ON SO SLOWLY,

WHILE OTHERS WILL FLY RIGHT ON BY.

I WILL GET TO TALK TO YOU OFTEN WHICH WILL BE GREAT!

I WILL TELL YOU WHAT I HAVE BEEN UP TO,
MY FAVORITE THINGS, AND HOW BIG I AM!

YOU MIGHT MISS SOME THINGS BUT THAT'S OK, BECAUSE I KNOW YOU ARE CHEERING ME ON FROM FAR AWAY.

WHEN TIME GETS CLOSER TO YOU COMING HOME, WE WILL BE GETTING EXCITED KNOWING THAT OUR "SEE YOU LATER" HAS FINALLY COME!

17

WAITING FOR YOU FOR WHAT SEEMS LIKE FOREVER MAKES IT
ALL WORTH IT WHEN I CAN GIVE YOU A BIG HUG!

SO NOW I UNDERSTAND WHY IT'S NOT GOODBYE, IT'S JUST
SOME WAITING UNTIL I SEE YOU LATER!

CPSIA information can be obtained
at www.ICGtesting.com
Printed in the USA
LVHW072208061119
636548LV00002B/35/P